Foreword

The behaviour and adventures of the characters in this book are modelled on those of certain actual meerkats still living in the Kalahari. These creatures wish to remain anonymous to protect their privacy. For this reason, their names and their language have been changed. Any similarity between these characters and any meerkat-stars of stage or screen is purely coincidental.
Furthermore, any resemblance between Oolooks or Whevubins on safari, actual Click-clicks or Sir David Attenborough is purely in the eye of the beholder.

Ian Whybrow

More Meerkat Madness

First published in Great Britain by HarperCollins *Children's Books* 2011
HarperCollins *Children's Books* is a division of HarperCollins*Publishers* Ltd,
77-85 Fulham Palace Road, Hammersmith, London W6 8JB

Visit us on the web at
www.harpercollins.co.uk

2

MORE MEERKAT MADNESS
Text copyright © Ian Whybrow 2011
Illustrations copyright © Sam Hearn 2011

Ian Whybrow asserts the moral right to be identified as the author of this work.

ISBN 978-0-00-744158-7

Printed and bound in England by
Clays Ltd, St Ives plc

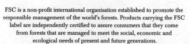

More Meerkat Madness

IAN WHYBROW

Illustrated by Sam Hearn

HarperCollins *Children's Books*

Also available by Ian Whybrow

Meerkat Madness

Little Wolf's Book of Badness

With thanks to Professor Tim Clutton-Brock who is responsible for much of the madness about meerkats and who has taught me – in fact, he has taught the nation as a whole – more about meerkats than Uncle Fearless has had barking geckos for breakfast.

Little Dream

Skeema

Down...

Deep down...

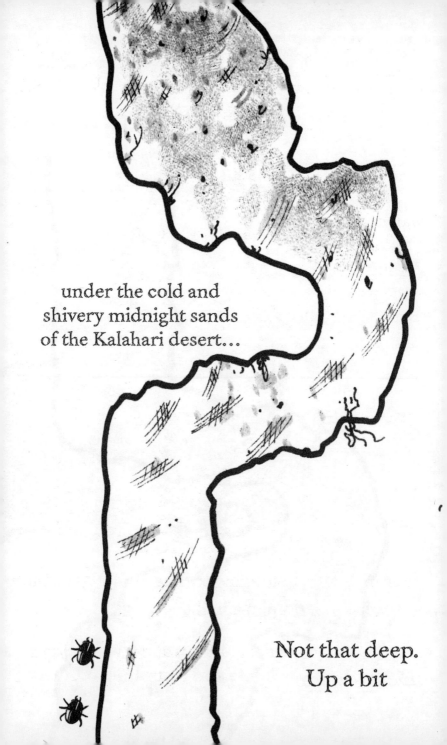

under the cold and
shivery midnight sands
of the Kalahari desert...

Not that deep.
Up a bit

Ah.
This is it.

Here, in the
warmest snuggest
of all warm,
snug sleeping
chambers of
Far Burrow,

four meerkats belonging to The Really Mad Mob
were rolled up in a ball.

This is the Meerkat Way to enjoy a
safe and restful sleep.

Chapter 1

Skeema, Mimi and Little Dream were thrilled
with their new home. Far Burrow was dark and
safe and wonderfully smelly. It was roomy, with
comfortable chambers and plenty
of secret entrances and exits.
Above all, it was *theirs* – a
home of their own that
they shared with their
dear old, mad old, lovely
old, one-eyed… Uncle
Fearless.

At the first coming of suntime, they made their way along the dark tunnels to the Upworld and stood together at the main entrance for Warm-up. Meerkats can't really get going until they have warmed up their minds and muscles properly. To do this, they have to point the little pads on their tummies towards the rising sun for a while. So there they were, tummy-pads in the air, feeling a bit shivery, a bit tired... but happy.

Uncle stood beside the kits, mumbling to himself. He had been doing this a lot just lately. In fact, lately he had become even more eccentric than usual. For example, he had taken to dashing off by himself for quite long periods. And he was always popping down into the burrow, even in the suntime, declaring that he was "just checking that all the escape tunnels were in good order, don't ya know?" If he had

16

checked them once, he had checked them more times than he had teeth and claws.

And now here he was, mumbling to himself: "Hmmm… get a grip, Fearless. Whup-whup, now! Not so much shilly-shallying, you fool! Get in there before it's too late. Just pop the question before she dashes off again, what-what…!"

"What *is* he muttering about?" whispered Mimi to Little Dream. "*…before she dashes off again…?*" Mimi usually thought of herself first and imagined that others did the same. "*She?* But I haven't dashed off anywhere lately, not me, not Mimi!"

Little Dream said nothing. He still hadn't woken up properly.

Uncle began to lick his paw and slick back his whiskers, *mmyim-mmyam*. "Quite honestly, Fearless, old boy, you're not looking too bad

17

for an old battler," he said aloud. "You may be a bit bent and bashed-up in places, but you've got your health and strength. So get on with it, laddy! Pounce before the beetle buries itself, as they say!"

Mimi's big brother, Skeema, pricked up his ears and looked sideways at Uncle. Being rather keen on plans and schemes himself, he too was curious to know what Fearless was up to. *"Pounce, eh?"* thought Skeema. *"Old battler…? Hmmm. I wonder if he's planning to have a fight with another meerkat mob. Prrrrr! Perhaps he's found out that the Ruddertails are planning another attack on Far Burrow!"*

For several suntimes now, Uncle had been exercising furiously. He had taken to doing press-ups, and making energetic sprints to and from a nearby shepherd tree. He would come back all breathless and fluttery, running his paws over his face and arms to smooth them and looking down to see if his fat tummy had got any smaller. Now and then he would throw himself on his back and kick all his legs in the air, making strange *yip-yip-wheeee!* noises and shouting, "I'm all yours! Come and get me!" He did a lot of waggling his eyebrows and clacking his teeth. Skeema felt pretty sure that he was getting himself fit for a scrap!

On this particular early-suntime, Uncle was taking unusual care with his grooming. He suddenly seemed to notice a wayward tuft in his fur and nibbled at it furiously. "Lie down tidy, now!" he growled. "Disgrace! This'll never do! Hmmm, nip nip! Must keep meself neat and handsome, what-what!"

"Aha! I get it!" said Skeema. He had suddenly

thought of another possibility. "Are you making yourself look nice for the Chief of the Click-clicks, Uncle?" he asked.

The Click-clicks were a small tribe of Blah-blahs who lived fairly close to Far Burrow. They were strange, giant creatures who had accepted Uncle as their king. They were not unlike monkeys, but smoother and they usually stayed out of trees and walked on the ground. They often came up quietly and left gifts of food for the Really Mad Mob. They bowed down to the meerkats and let them climb up on to their heads. Being as tall as young thorn trees, they made excellent look-out posts.

To show how much he admired Uncle, the Chief of the Click-clicks had given him the special collar that he always wore with pride. Like all Blah-blahs, the Click-clicks talked in *blah-blah-blah* noises instead of squeaking and chattering to one another in the normal way. The only time they didn't go *blah-blah-blah* was when they got excited. Then they sounded like hyenas… *hee-hee-ha-ha-haaah!*

The Click-clicks had plenty of strange and silly habits. For example, instead of building proper, safe burrows deep down under the sands, they made pointy white mounds *above the ground*! These were so flimsy that you could see them flapping whenever the wind blew. The Click-click tribe was so called because they were very shy and often hid their eyes behind special eye-protectors whenever they came to

 admire the meerkats up close – which was often. Sometimes they used their tongues to make *click-click* noises as a greeting.

"No, no. The Click-clicks have gone, I'm afraid," said Uncle, staring outwards. "The rains will be here soon; I can smell 'em. And Blah-blahs get very nervous about storms, don't you know. Those feeble pointy mounds of theirs won't keep them safe from sky-crash and fizz-fire. That's why they've all jumped into their Vroom-vrooms, d'you see? I expect they've gone to find a safer place to live."

The Click-clicks were not clever enough to think of building lots of different escape-tunnels. Instead, they relied on enormous travelling burrows that moved on spinners. At the first

sign of danger, they would jump into them and
vroom-vroom! – off they would roar in a cloud
of dust.

"Oh, dear! That means no more nuts and
eggs for me-me, then," sighed Mimi. "No more
standing on their heads and having my tummy
tickled."

At the mention of the word *tummy*, Uncle

slid his paws under his rather fat one and hoisted
it up with a "One-two-three… HUP!" It was a
habit of his. Skeema and Mimi giggled and did a
"One-two-three… HUP!" immitation of him. He
took no notice, and just kept on gazing into the
distance, sighing. After a while he sang a little
ditty to himself:

"Fleabites are red, my love.

Blue skinks are blue.

Lizards are yummy, love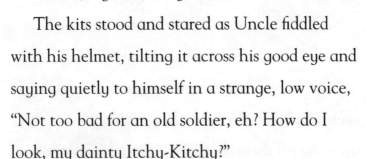

And so, my fluff, are you."

The kits stood and stared as Uncle fiddled
with his helmet, tilting it across his good eye and
saying quietly to himself in a strange, low voice,
"Not too bad for an old soldier, eh? How do I
look, my dainty Itchy-Kitchy?"

"You don't think he's going potty, do you,
Skeema?" said Mimi.

"I hope not," said Skeema. "Although, come to think of it, he has been doing some very peculiar things lately. He kept me awake for ages in the darktime, talking in his sleep, giving me hard squeezes and saying strange things to me in a soppy sort of voice."

"What sort of things?" asked Mimi.

"Well… like: *You'll be quite safe with me, you fabulous creature.*"

"What do you think he's on about?" said Mimi.

At that moment, Mimi heard something behind her and, turning round quickly, saw something moving in the shadows. She let out such a dreadful shriek that Little Dream leaped up and gave a shriek himself.

"WUP! WUP! WUP! ACTION STATIONS!" cried Mimi.

"Wh-what?" growled Uncle. "Enemies, is it?

TAKE COVER! DIVE-DIVE-DIVE!"

In one sweeping movement, Skeema grabbed his trusty lime-green Snap-snap – a powerful weapon he had acquired from the Click-click tribe – and held him at the ready.

Tails up, claws out, the kits braced themselves, ready to run to safety or fight for their lives.

For a moment they stood rooted to the spot, for there, behind them, something was making its way steadily towards them from the darkness of their very own burrow!

Chapter 2

What was it, struggling up out of the gloom? A honey badger? A cobra? Either could be deadly!

Suddenly Uncle let out his breath and relaxed. "Stand easy, the Really Mads!" he ordered. "No danger."

He bustled past the kits, bowed deeply into the tunnel and offered a helping paw to the intruder. "Up we come," he said.

The stranger was a fabulously fluffy female meerkat. She was tall and youthful, and when she turned, she showed very pretty, regularly-spaced dark patches down the sandy fur of her back. She had clearly lost weight and condition, but not her dignity. Her eyes were very deep and dark and her gaze was steady. When she saw how anxiously the kits looked at her, she almost turned and went back the way she had come. But then she seemed to check herself and stepped forward and spoke up boldly. "What ho, Fearless, old thing," she said. She sounded very grand and hearty. "I hope this isn't an awkward moment. But I really don't think I can keep myself a secret for much longer. There! I've done it now, haven't I?"

With that, she threw herself down on to her tummy in the still-cold sand in the way respectful meerkats have when they wish to be introduced.

"Now, now, m'dear! Get to your paws, please!" said Uncle, puffing his chest out, pulling in his tummy and straightening his safari scarf. "No need for ceremony! The kits are not going to bite you. You're quite safe here with us. Come out and join our Warm-up."

"What is *she* doing near me, Mimi, in my home?" exclaimed Mimi indignantly.

"*Our* home," corrected Little Dream quietly, looking a little confused.

Skeema dashed over and peered down into the entrance tunnel, wagging his bottom from side to side as fiercely as he could, to show that he was ready for any sort of attack. "If there are any

more of you down there – come out and fight!"
he cried.

Mimi joined him, and began to make loud
spit-calls to show how fierce she was. "Yes! Come
out and fight me, me!" she challenged. "I'm
special, you know! I'm the maddest kit of all the
Really Mads!"

Little Dream was still looking rather dazed
by the speed at which things were happening,
but he was quick to stand shoulder to shoulder
with his brother and sister. "Exactly," he cried.
It wasn't very scary but it was the best he could
manage on the spur of the moment.

"Steady! As you were, everyone!" growled
Uncle Fearless. "Stand easy! There's no-one else
down there, you can take my word for it."

"There could be, Uncle!" said Skeema. "After
all, this female must have sneaked in through

one of the escape-tunnels." Skeema knew a trick or too himself so he was always quick to sniff out the cunning plans of others.

"I can assure you, Skeema," said Uncle, licking his paw and briskly polishing the fur on his chest with it, "that I invited only one guest to use the spare chamber last night. And that was Miss – or to use her proper title, hem-hem – *Princess* – Radiant."

At the word *princess*, Mimi bristled. She had always wanted to be a princess like her poor mother, Princess Fragrant who, tragically, had disappeared when Mimi and her brothers were no bigger than baby mole-rats. So when the Really Mad Mob had moved to Far Burrow, Uncle had promised Mimi she could be a princess. Thanks to Uncle Fearless, they had escaped from their old home where they had been bullied by cold

Queen Heartless and her horrid, mean royal kits.

They had made their way, facing any number of dangers together, across the kingdom of the Sharpeyes, almost as far as the land of their arch-rivals, the fearsome Ruddertails. Mimi no longer had to bow and scrape to the cruel Princess Dangerous, who had reminded her constantly that she and her brothers were of no importance at all, being mere orphans.

Now the Really Mads had their *own* burrow and their *own* tribe, and she certainly didn't want to have to go through *that* sort of thing again!

Skeema was still alarmed too, and he blurted out, "Is she a Ruddertail? She smells like one to me."

"Enemies!" piped Little Dream, remembering the tremendous fight they had all had to keep the Ruddertails out of Far Burrow when they first arrived.

"Manners, everyone!" roared Uncle. "Silence, PLEASE!" Sulkily, the kits obeyed. He went on, "Princess Radiant is most certainly not a Ruddertail, Skeema. And she is not an enemy. She is... or rather she *was*... a member of the Truepatch tribe, who treated her as cruelly as the Sharpeyes treated us. *And* they threw her out. Sadly for her, she had no fellow meerkats with her, so had no choice for many a suntime and darktime but to be a tribeless Wanderer. When I came across her, worn-out and defenceless under a shrub on the border of Shepherd Tree Clump, I... well, I didn't hesitate, did I, Princess?"

"Radiant, please, my dear! Let the kitties just call me Radiant!"

"Kitties!" spluttered Mimi. "Me? Me? A *kitty*?"

Uncle ignored Mimi and pressed on with

his story. "I had no hesitation in offering the, *hurrumph*, very lovely Radiant, my protection. *Our* protection, I should say. Only…"

"Only we thought I might be a bit of a shock to you if I just wandered into the burrow," put in Radiant with a twitch of her (very lovely) nose. "So we thought I'd better lie low until we could think of a way of, er, breaking the news about me as gently as possible. Your uncle – the dear, kind fellow – hid me away and brought me all sorts of

smashing grub to fatten me up a bit. Didn't you,
my splendid old fearless hero?"

The kits looked at each other and rolled their
eyes. "Yuck!" muttered Mimi.

"That explains why Uncle kept running off and
disappearing!" whispered Skeema with a touch
of admiration. "And why he kept pretending to
check on the escape-tunnels. Crafty!"

"But she can't stay *here*," returned Mimi,
horrified.

"Well, I don't want to intrude if I'm not wanted," said the newcomer, sensing that she was far from welcome. "Perhaps I should leave now. I'm sorry…"

"Nonsense! You're not intruding at all!" cried Uncle. "Allow me to introduce you properly. Radiant, this is my niece, Mimi. Say how-do-you-do, Mimi."

Mimi was so furious that she could only *just* manage to say hello.

Skeema was equally stiff and he couldn't quite bring himself to say that he was pleased to meet her.

Little Dream was much more welcoming. "How do you do?" he said politely and touched his nose against the stranger's face. "Our Mama is a Wanderer too," he said sadly. "I have dreams about her sometimes. Her name's Fragrant. You didn't bump into her on your wanderings, did you, by any chance?"

"Now, now, Dreamie," said Uncle gently. "Let's not go over that again, eh, dear boy?" His sister, Fragrant, was dead and gone, he was sure of it. He hated to see the little chap get excited by a false hope. "*Harrumph!* I tell you what. We can't bring your Mama back. But I've been thinking. What the Really Mad Mob needs more than anything is – um – a kind and caring adult female to join us. Someone strong, with spirit, d'you see? Someone who can bring... well, the things that the right sort of adult females can bring."

"But *you* look after us," said Skeema.

"And we manage very well on our own," grumbled Mimi.

Uncle wasn't listening. He gazed adoringly at Radiant. "So if you'll permit me, my dear..." he said, "as King of the Really Mads,

37

and Lord of the Click-clicks – I should like to welcome you officially into our tribe."

In a flash, he twirled like a dancer and sprayed her with the mark of the Really Mad Mob. "Please consider yourself one of us," he said merrily, rapidly blinking his one good eye. "Kits, give her a nice welcome, what-what!" He puffed out his chest proudly.

"I say, you're all *frightfully* decent!" cried Radiant, hugging them firmly and giving everyone a jolly good nose-rub. "I can't tell you how grateful I am to be among friends and out of danger. I had a pretty grim time all on my own-io in the Upworld, I don't mind telling you. We meerkats are not much good without other meerkats looking out for us, are we?" She tried to make light of it, but were those tears of relief shining in her eyes? She wiped them away impatiently. "I'm not sure how I can ever thank you." She looked hard at Uncle when she said this. Then she was bustling among the kits, squeezing and nipping them affectionately. "But I give you my word that I am bally-well going to try."

Skeema and Mimi managed to mumble something and Uncle, bursting with joy and pride, gathered them all into his arms.

"Hear, hear," said Little Dream, politely. "Good speech. Welcome to the Really Mads."

Chapter 3

"Now, come along, everyone!" Uncle cried.
"That's enough talk! With the rains so late, we
need to save bags of energy just to find enough
to eat. Tails up then, the Really Mads, and let's
head for the foraging grounds!"

Off they raced, dipping in and out of the dry
tufts of spiky grass splashed with the stinking
white tell-tale scent-marks of hyenas. "Eyes
sharp!" barked Uncle Fearless. "Stay together to
stay alive! Don't be fooled just because hyenas
giggle. The louder they laugh, the hungrier they

are." So everyone was extra-watchful as they came to open ground near a lofty camelthorn tree.

"I'll take first sentry-duty!" cried Mimi in a huffy sort of voice. She darted up to the top of the tree like a monkey and scanned the horizon for signs of trouble. "Though why I should look out for HER I really don't know," she muttered under her breath.

With Mimi on guard, the others could get their heads down and dig with a will, but the pickings were thin. Before the rains came, food was always scarce. The damp places, where the juiciest bugs and lizards and scorpions love to cool themselves, lay far below the surface and were hard to sniff out.

Skeema was chasing ants, throwing up a shower of hot sand to get at some of their eggs, when he suddenly came face to face with a crawler he hadn't met before. It was a shiny black beetle with white marks on its cheeks. It seemed to be tucking into the ants itself and was waving its long legs and pincers in a wild sort of way. Skeema was very fond of his food, especially scorpions, so he was used to the darting and threatening tricks that many delicious creatures use to try to avoid getting eaten. In fact, the sheer cheek of the little creature made him determined to find out what it tasted like. He lowered his nose almost to the ground to get within nibbling range. Then he began to knock the beetle about with his paw.

Crack-crack! The creature let off a double explosion from its back end! It sent twin streams of acid flying right at Skeema's eye! With a yelp

and a backward-roll, Skeema flung himself away
from the danger. But in a couple of seconds he
was nose down and back in the hunt.

"Careful now!" warned Uncle. "Black-and-
white stranger – always a danger! I've told you
that before. That's an Oogpister you're playing
with, by all that stinks and stings! He'll do real
damage to your eyes if you let him! Give him a
wide berth!"

43

"Respect!" muttered Skeema to the little squirt, thinking how clever it was and that, if ever he found himself cornered, a quick Oogpister-move, might come in very handy.

When it was Skeema's turn to keep watch, Mimi came down from her perch to feed. She was still very grumpy and complained to Little Dream, "I'm not hungry at all, and it's all Uncle's fault!"

She was dreadfully jealous. Instead of giving her lots of attention, Uncle seemed to be more or less ignoring her. He kept fussing after Radiant, offering her the choicest grubs and crawlers, no matter how difficult they were to find.

Mimi stamped about in a sulk, scratching at the increasingly hot sand and throwing it up in clouds when she could find nothing to eat.

Radiant noticed what was going on and

44

trotted over to her with a fat skink between her jaws – a rare find in this dry season and one of Mimi's favourites. "Here," she said kindly. "You have it. You've done a lovely job as look-out. You must be starving, you poor thing."

But Mimi was in a shocking temper by now. "I am not poor and I am not *your* anything!" she announced.

"Oh, right! Fine!" said Radiant, trying her best to pretend that she wasn't deeply hurt by this outburst, "I was only going to give you a tip about finding a bit of juice when things are frightfully dry, that's all. I stumbled on this little trick on my wanderings. Let me show you. What you do is, you find a shrub. Doesn't matter how dead-looking it is. You work out where its roots might be running to and then you dig quite deep..."

"I *know* where to dig," said Mimi with a haughty sniff. "Leave me alone."

"Now look here," said Radiant kindly but firmly. "Adults are not always right, but they sometime have valuable experience that's worth passing on. Kits should pay attention to adults. That's how they learn. That's the Meerkat Way."

"I want Uncle to teach me the Meerkat Way, not a stranger!"

Radiant nudged the skink with her nose. "You're hungry," she said. "You're upset. I suggest you eat this. It'll make you feel better. But I'm officially a member of this tribe too now, Mimi, so I think you should make an effort to be a little more respectful to me."

And with that she turned and made her way back to the burrow, obviously rather shaken.

Uncle trotted over. "Radiant, my dear!" he called. "Is anything the matter? Are you all right? Wait up, what-what!" And he scampered after her.

*

Little Dream and Skeema walked over to Mimi, who was standing on her own, looking very cross indeed.

"It's true what Radiant says about meerkats needing to look out for one another, Mimi," said Little Dream. "Stay together to stay alive, remember?" he said, reciting the mob's motto.

"Then Uncle should be staying together with us then!" sniffed Mimi, beginning to cry, "Not running around after *females*."

Little Dream was anxious to comfort her. "Yes, but he did help us escape from our birth-burrow, and we all hated *that*, didn't we?" he said. "And

47

he brought us safely across to this lovely spot on the far side of the Upworld!"

"Well said, Dreamy!" agreed Skeema. "No more bowing and scraping to nasty Queen Heartless and her horrid kits! We got away from her – and we have Uncle to thank for that!" He gave his Snap-snap a squeeze that made it squeak loudly and defiantly.

"Good old Uncle!" cried Little Dream. "And when you come to think of it, what happened to Radiant is just like what happened to Mama, isn't it?" he went on. "I mean to say, it's like when Queen Heartless got jealous of Mama and chased her out of the burrow, isn't it?"

Little Dream had worked himself up by now. "I feel sure Mama's still alive!" he declared. "She's become a Wanderer like Radiant used to be. It's horrible to think of her all alone in the desert with no one to help her keep watch for enemies!" His eyes grew wide and full of tears.

Skeema decided that a quick play-fight might cheer his little brother up a bit. "Come on, Dreamie," he said fondly. "Let's not go over all that again." And he bundled him over a couple of times and chewed a tick off his ear, for luck.

Chapter 4

The following suntime, Warm-up started as a very frosty affair. Mimi still refused to speak to Radiant, so as soon as his tummy-pad started getting toasty, Uncle tried to smooth things over by being extra-cheery.

"Well, I must say I slept like a jelly-melon!" he bellowed. "I feel as frisky as a dung-beetle in a warthog-wallow, by all that's fresh and jolly. What about you, Radiant, my dear? Was there plenty of spring in the nesting-material in the spare chamber?"

"Tickety-boo, I thank you, Your Royal

Highness-and-Lowness!" said Radiant, chuckling. "Never slept better in my life."

"Now, now, no titles, no titles, or I shall have to start calling you Princess again!" said Uncle. "And how about you, kits? Mimi? Skeema? Are you quite refreshed?"

"Well, at least you weren't talking in your sleep again, Uncle," said Skeema cheekily. "But I must say, Dreamy was horribly wriggly."

They all looked over at Little Dream, who was swaying from side to side, then suddenly, without warning, fell flat on his nose, fast asleep again.

Skeema helped him up again. "I'm not surprised you're so tired," he said, giving him a dust-down. "What was up? Were you having a nightmare or something?"

"Sorry," said Little Dream, rubbing his nose. "I thought I heard Mama again. She was calling out. She kept saying: *Come and find me! Bring me home! Follow the pawprints!* And I ran and I ran and I looked and I looked and for a long time there was just sand. And then I found some prints leading far away… and then I woke up."

"Never mind, old chap! Nothing to worry about. It was only a dream, " said Uncle, giving him a squeeze. "Let's go out hunting, eh? Give ourselves a good shake-up! That'll put us right as reptiles, what-what!"

"You poor little mite," said Radiant, with real feeling. "You must

52

miss your mother terribly."

"What about me, me?" cried Mimi, breaking her sulky silence. "*I* miss her as well, you know!"

"Of course you do," said Radiant quickly. "I didn't mean…"

"Now, Mimi!" snapped Uncle. "I won't have this constant rudeness to our newest member! You just start thinking about others, don't you know!"

"Uncle," said Skeema, anxious to avoid a nasty row, "about Mama… On the night that Queen Heartless made her leave the burrow… is it… are you absolutely *certain* that she died?"

"Well… I… I hardly know how to answer you, my boy," said Uncle. "I really think we should try to move on. We all miss Fragrant, of course we do. Your mama was one of the finest females among the Sharpeyes, one of the bravest and most tender. But we have to face facts, yes – yes?

53

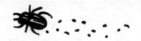

When Heartless expelled your mama from her birth-burrow, there were wild dogs about. And jackals too. I heard them myself, yapping for blood. I'm afraid that she had very little chance of escaping them all, not by herself."

Little Dream was suddenly so alert that he was quivering. "You said *very little* chance, Uncle. You didn't say there was *no* chance."

"But, my dear Dreamie…"

"Were the wild dogs and jackals close by the burrow or far away?" said Little Dream, pressing on.

"I can't honestly say," said Uncle. "I was deep below the ground in the nursery chamber, being a baby-sitter to you kits."

"Aha!" exclaimed Little Dream. "If you were deep down, how could you be sure…?"

"What I'm saying, dear boy, is that there

54

were certainly some pretty fearsome brutes on the loose when your poor mama was chased out into the Upworld. I simply don't see how it would have been possible for her – for *any* lone meerkat – to defend herself against a ruthless and cunning pack."

"Your uncle's right, you know," put in Radiant gently. "But I'm sure she didn't suffer. The end would have come very quickly. That's something, isn't it?"

Uncle was visibly touched by her support. He cleared his throat. "Harrumph! Come along now, everyone. We need *action*! Brace up and wup-wup! Ready for your breakfast? I must say, I'm very anxious to show Radiant our foraging-ground over by Kudu Ridge. Are you all set? Best paws forwards and off we go, then! Yip-yip! Tally-ho!"

"Tally-ho!" cried Radiant. "I could eat an aardvark!"

She and Uncle skipped on ahead, looking back encouragingly at the kits every now and then, playfully bumping into each other as they went. Skeema and Mimi fell in behind them, a little more glumly, but looking forward to breakfast, at least.

Little Dream, however, was still lagging behind.

"Come on, Dreamie," said Skeema. "Let's go and dig up something wiggly!"

"You go ahead," he told his brother and sister, his eyes shining. "I'm going to find Mama!"

And with that, he scrambled up the steep side of the sand dune that towered above the well-trodden path to the foraging grounds. He reached the top and gazed down at the chain of salt pans that stretched away to the west beyond

the dry riverbed like huge, dark lily pads.

"Wait for me! Me! I'm coming with you! I won't stay here a moment longer with that dreadful female!" Mimi declared and scrambled after him.

Skeema was alarmed. "Where are you going? Stay together to stay alive, remember?" he warned. And just to underline the point, at that moment, a martial eagle flapped from its perch high in a quiver tree.

Distracted as he was by the delightful company of his lively new female friend, and in spite of having only one eye, Uncle was quick to see the danger and to sound the alert. "TAKE COVER, EVERYONE! DIVE! DIVE! DIVE!" he ordered, and in a flurry of dust, wrestled Radiant into the nearest bolt-hole.

For a moment Skeema span round like a cornered ground squirrel, not knowing where to turn. "Wup-wup! Look out, Little Dream! Stop, Mimi!" he urged. But Mimi and Little Dream were out of sight, over the ridge now. Seeing that Uncle and Radiant were safely underground, and praying that the eagle's attention was not on him, he dashed after his brother and sister as fast as terror and legs could move him, his brave tail waving like a flag.

Chapter 5

When Skeema caught up with Little Dream and Mimi, they were standing at the margin of a grey and dried-out salt pan, gazing out at a grass-covered rocky hill in the distance that rose up out of the desert sands.

"Like a green island," muttered Little Dream, in a daze. Then, casting his eyes downwards, he noticed some marks that had been newly pressed into the dark crust beneath them. These made a line into the distance as far as even meerkat eyes could see. "Pawprints!" he exclaimed, looking up at the others. "Just like in my dream!"

"These aren't Mama's prints," panted Skeema.

"They can't be." He lowered his head and sniffed. "These are enemy pawprints – a cat's, by the looks of them." He sniffed again. "Small enough to be a cheetah's or a leopard's… but no, a lion's I think. He's not a big one, but big enough to have the lot of us for breakfast, anyway."

"But these are the same pawprints from my dream, I'm sure! Maybe he's carrying Mama off somewhere to eat her?" cried Little Dream. "We've no time to lose!"

"This is ridiculous!" complained Skeema. "You're letting your imagination run away with you!"

But Little Dream paid no attention. He dashed off again, the salty crust crackling under his paws. Mimi and Skeema shook their heads in disbelief, but scrambled after him anyway.

As the sun rose in the sky, the Upworld began to shimmer in the growing heat. Having tracked the pawprints all morning, the meerkats suddenly noticed that they had stopped going in a straight line, drifting off first to the left, then to the right. "Whoever's been leaving these tracks must have been getting tired," muttered Skeema. On they went, and more than once the prints went round in a circle. But then the pawprints steadied, and eventually led the little band of meerkats straight to the green island they had spotted in the distance earlier. Then the pawprints disappeared.

"Now what do we do?" panted Mimi. "This lion – or whatever it is that we've been following – he could be hiding around here somewhere. Supposing he pounces on me!"

"On *us*," said her brother wearily. "And, I'm sorry, Dreamie, but I really don't see the point of all this. OK, it might make sense to follow *meerkat*-prints, because then at least there's a *faint* possibly that they could have been left by Mama, but—"

"But these are the prints I saw in my dream,

when I heard Mama calling!" insisted Dreamy.

"Yes, well, she's not calling now," said Mimi sourly. A cluster of blots on the cloudless blue sky suddenly caught the kits' attention.

"Look out!" warned Skeema. "More sky-enemies!" Above the crest of the hill where trees grew tall and green in spite of the baking heat, ugly shapes circled on lazy wings. The kits dived for cover among some spiny drie-doring bushes on the lower slopes and got their breath back.

"What are they?" whispered Mimi. "Please don't let them be what I think they are…!"

"Vultures!" whispered Skeema after a while.

"Thank goodness! They're not after me, then!" said Mimi with a sigh of relief. "Phew! I thought they were The Silent Enemy."

Eagle-owls – feared by all meerkats – held a special terror for the Really Mad Mob because of

63

what one of them had done to Uncle long ago, when he had been King of the Sharpeyes. He forgot to watch the sky for a split second. The Silent Enemy had swooped down, snatched him into the air and pecked out his eye!

Fearless by name, fearless by nature, Uncle had put up a heroic fight and forced the bird to drop him. But he had fallen from a great height and broken several bones. Having somehow managed to crawl back to the safety of his burrow, he soon fell into a fever and then into the dreaded Meerkat Madness! Not one meerkat in his tribe expected him to live. And when he did recover his senses, it was to find that he was no longer King. His sneaking brother, Chancer, had taken his place and married his wife, Queen Heartless, whilst he lay panting in his sick bed. So when at last he did come to his senses, he found himself reduced to the rank of… babysitter.

This was how he had come to be given the care of Skeema Mimi and Little Dream when their mother had been cast out into exile in the Upworld. Bitterly unhappy with their harsh treatment by the Sharpeyes, Uncle and the kits had managed to escape and begin a blissful new life under a new name in a far-away burrow. Blissful, that is, until just lately.

"Vultures always mean that something's dead – or dying," said Skeema. "Maybe it's the cat."

"Or Mama!" said Little Dream, his eyes wide with terror. "We must find her!"

Skeema and Mimi both thought he was barmy, but they could see that there was no stopping him. They clambered up the hill as quietly as they could, trying to keep under cover and always sniffing for a hint of the trail of the cat they were stalking. Gradually, the low, flat rocks gave way to taller boulders, and when they looked up they saw a line of trees and tall, yellowish cliffs beyond them.

Soon the sheltering bushes gave way to whispering pygmy grass. When the kits dived into it to take cover, they found themselves in a sort of maze, criss-crossed by the pathways of

mice and snakes. They pressed through, nervous
of cobras and puff-adders. Then, in order to
reach the shade of the trees, they were forced
to dash out into open ground again and leap
from one hot rock to another. Crickets and

grasshoppers flicked past them, and monarch
butterflies swooped and dipped. Over their heads,
parrots and birds of every colour of the rainbow
flapped and chattered.

Once or twice they encountered creatures disguised as twigs and leaves. "Nice try!" said Skeema as he swallowed a bug that was pretending to be a small stone. "But your mama should have taught you not to wriggle. Yum!" He smacked his lips and put the idea into his memory-bank. *When danger comes and you can't find a bolt-hole, stand still as a stone near something the same colour as you.*

After walking on a while, they found themselves darting among the trunks of ancient trees. Suddenly they entered a sheltered space between the trees and the cliffs. The clearing was curved like a creature sleeping on its side, with the outstretched legs formed by low flat rocks worn smooth by the backsides of generations of ancient Blah-blahs who sometimes came here to live secretly when times were too hard in the desert.

"What is this place?" said Little Dream, looking around in awe.

It was certainly unlike any place they had ever seen, but they were more wary than charmed by it. Ears, eyes, noses, whiskers – everything was on full-alert.

The ground was cool and trodden flat, always shaded by the trees, or by the shadow of the wall of cliff that rose up along the back.

"FIRE!" hissed Skeema suddenly. He didn't need to shout because Mimi and Little Dream had smelled the danger too and were standing quite still, looking around for smoke and flames, ready to jump to safety.

But the fire was not one that leapt and killed you. It was a small dead one, caged by round stones and turned to ash. In the middle of it was the blackened hind leg of a large animal.

Mimi, who was starving, took a little nibble at
it and found there was goodness under the burnt
shell. The others had a little taste and were soon
feeling stronger and bolder. Then they decided to
spread out and explore.

It wasn't long before their noses led them to
something buried in a cool patch of sand and
hidden under scattered leaves. Little Dream
scrabbled with his digging-claws and uncovered
two enormous oval shapes that were almost as
big as him. They had been buried standing up.

"Ostrich eggs!" laughed Skeema.

"Yes, but they have been opened and re-
sealed!" said Mimi. "Look what's inside!" She
put her claws into a narrow crack and pulled the
top off one of the eggs. "Water!" she exclaimed.
"It's fresh and cool and sweet. Taste it!" But the
others were too excited and scuttled about to see

70

what other treasures they could find, so she put the top back on and re-buried the egg-wells.

And all the time, wide, keen eyes were watching from high in the branches of a tree. A boy (we shall call him Shadow, for he was as dark as a shadow) sat licking honey from his fingers. He did it slowly and carefully so that his white teeth would not shine and even his pink tongue stayed a secret. Wild bees buzzed round him and some were angry enough with him for stealing their honey to sting him, but still he did not move a muscle.

He was curious to see what other things of his the meerkats would discover for themselves, and also – what would happen when the lion cub saw them.

Chapter 6

While Mimi sniffed among the nut shells and fruit skins that were scattered round the fire, Skeema's attention was taken by a bunch of pretty feathers and porcupine quills and some thin hollow bones that lay further off. There were also some skins, soft as rabbits' fur, lying about. "Springhares," thought Skeema, remembering the way they sometimes *pronked*, like crazy little springboks, past the entrance to Far Burrow as darktime was falling. "Fast," he thought, "but obviously not fast enough."

Mimi found a little string of white beads – she had seen a female Click-click wearing something like this round her neck! She tried it on. It fitted her head perfectly! She also found a little pouch made of soft animal skin. It was decorated with shiny bits of smooth glass and sewn together with fine woven grass. She peeked into it, thinking that perhaps she might find something to eat. In fact, it was full of little bits of broken ostrich shell, all brightly painted in different colours. Together they shone like feathers on a Kalahari kingfisher.

Skeema stifled a little cry as he discovered a parcel, made of a folded broad leaf in which was wrapped fat caterpillars, some fresh roots and tubers, full of juice, and a batch of tiny weaver-bird eggs. He cracked one and sucked it dry. Delicious! He thought about telling Mimi what he had discovered, but when he looked across and saw that she was chewing at something, it gave him a good excuse to be greedy and keep quiet.

The pouch, it seemed, had a horrid, bitter taste. Mimi began to cough and spit.

"Come up here!" called Little Dream. "I've found something wonderful! And you can cool your tongue, Mimi!"

Mimi and Skeema saw that he was up on a ledge where a thorn hedge was growing against the cliff. They followed a little path up to where Little Dream was, and found that he had discovered some rocks that oozed water.

Meerkats can do without water, so long as there's plenty of juice in what

74

they eat – but when they find it, they're always thankful for a drink. Gratefully, Mimi ran her tongue over the dripping moss and got rid of the horrid taste.

"I found some running water further up the cliff," said Little Dream. "It bubbles up from the rocks there – but this is lovely to lick, isn't it? And look here…" He led them behind the thorn hedge and showed them the entrance to a cave. The smooth, gold-coloured walls were bright with red shapes outlined in black. "What do those shapes remind you of?" he asked.

"That one looks like a teeny giraffe!" said Mimi. "And there's a wildebeest – and an elephant…"

"And some pronking springbok, look!" added Little Dream. "And hippos, and a porcupine…"

"I can't see me, me!" said Mimi. "Can anyone

see a meerkat?" She was disappointed not to find
a single one.

"I like that shape that looks like a Blah-blah
with a sharp stick!" cried Skeema, ignoring her.

They were enchanted. They thought they
were very clever to be able to see animals in the
black-and-red shapes on the walls. They thought
they were a beautiful accident. They had no idea
that they had been painted specially by a boy

who carried a spear, who loved to make beads
from bits of glass and broken ostrich shell – a boy
who respected all creatures and wished to learn
from them – who thought it was fair to be stung
by bees if you stole their honey.

The kits stood in a sort of trance – which is
why they almost jumped out of their skins when
they heard a low growl from somewhere deep
inside the cave.

Chapter 7

"LION!" screamed Mimi. "Let's get out of here!"

Mimi and Skeema rushed back to the cave-entrance but Little Dream didn't move.

"Wup-wup! Run for your life, Dreamie!" urged Skeema.

"Hush!" said Little Dream, and he was so calm and determined and serious that even in their panic, Mimi and Skeema stood quiet and still.

"Mama!" rumbled the voice. It sounded very weak. "Help me."

"It's a trick!" cried Skeema. "Take no notice!"

"We've followed him all this way," said Little Dream. "He's calling for Mama. She must be around somewhere." And he rushed into the darkness.

"It's HIS mama he wants, not ours, you silly thing!" wailed Skeema. But when they realised that Little Dream was putting himself in danger, he and Mimi rushed to support him. Their war cries – and the shrill squeaks that the Snap-snap made as Skeema held him up and squeezed him – sounded extra-loud and fearsome in the echoing gloom of the cave.

As it turned out, the lion cub had not the strength to crawl, let alone to plan a meerkat supper. He lay on his side, with hardly a spark of life in the slits of his poor bloodshot eyes. His tongue lolled from his mouth. He only had breath in him to pant, and none left over to

answer a single question.

"Look how thin he is. He's starving," murmured Mimi. "He needs food."

"Yes, but look at the size of him!" warned Skeema. "Look at his claws! Look how big his mouth is! He could swallow us all in one go!"

"He's too weak," said Mimi. There was pity in her voice. "And he's only a kit like me, really."

"Like us," chorused her brothers.

Little Dream had a suggestion. "Why don't we feed him, then run away – and then ask him if he can tell us anything about Mama?"

"That is a totally nutty idea, Dreamie!" scoffed Skeema. "How can we run away and then ask him questions?"

"Oh," said Little Dream, feeling foolish. "I didn't mean a *long* way away."

"Listen, I agree that we ought to try

to find out what he's doing here," Skeema went on. "And he's not going to last much longer if we don't get some food into him. But what are we going to feed him?"

"The meat!" cried Mimi, remembering the blackened leg in the ashes down below. "Come on, everyone!"

The kits skittered down the rocky path to the clearing and tried to lift the leg that had been cooked in the fire, but it was too heavy to carry, even for the three of them at once.

"It's no good. We'll just have to take him some eggs," said Skeema, adding a little sheepishly that he had come across a small hoard of them earlier.

"Well, you're the oldest," Mimi reminded Skeema. "You take some to him."

"I'm only the oldest by a few heartbeats!" he responded.

"Yes, but you're the fastest. Run over and put an egg down under his nose."

Skeema hesitated.

"I *dare* you," urged Mimi.

That did it. He couldn't resist a dare. "Here goes," he whispered. "Wish me luck!" And off he scampered on his mission.

*

For a second the cub's eyelids flickered. That stopped Skeema in his tracks. Then the cub's nostrils opened and closed. Then he was still.

"He's out cold," said Skeema, letting his breath out in a rush of relief. "I think the only thing for it is for one of us to hold his mouth open while the others feed him."

"Good idea," agreed Little Dream. "B-but who's going to…?"

"Oh, come on – I'll do it," said Skeema. "You

bring some more eggs." He tip-toed forward a few paces. Stopped. Took a deep breath. Raised his front paws over his head and did a little hip-wiggling shimmy. Mimi and Little Dream got ready to drop their eggs and run.

Nothing. Not a twitch.

"Stand by," whispered Skeema. He stood with his back to the cub's slack mouth, put his feet on the bottom jaw and heaved up against the top jaw like a little weight-lifter, straining every muscle.

Bit by bit, the mouth split open revealing scarily sharp teeth.

"Go for it!" urged Skeema, and Mimi and Little Dream cracked a couple of eggs on his bottom fangs. Quickly they smeared the sticky goodness all over his dry, swollen tongue. "Jump back!" yelled Skeema and sprang free himself, as the jaws snapped shut.

That seemed to do the trick at once. The cub began to suck and smack his lips like a new-born taking milk from its mother. Patiently, bravely, the team carried on feeding him. After a long while they managed to get him to swallow all the eggs and even the caterpillars. He began to stir a little and soon he had the strength to spit out the bulbs and tubers that the kits popped into his mouth. "Yuck!" he groaned.

The kits fled to a safe distance. There was a

pause and then Mimi said. "You should eat your vegetables."

"Hush, Mimi," said Skeema. "He's a carnivore, you know, not an omnivore like us!" Then he added kindly to the cub, "can you get up now?"

He got a groan for an answer, but that was something.

"Come along," said Little Dream. "Get up and we'll take you to some water. Do you promise not to eat us?"

"Hmmmm," rumbled the cub, and they took that for a yes.

They crawled underneath the cub's belly and jogged and nudged and nipped and tickled him until at last he struggled on to his pads. Then they jostled and tugged him by his ears until they got him outside by the dripping rocks, where slowly and with some difficulty, the little cub lapped up some of the moisture. That put a little more of a spark into him and slowly, patiently, they led him down the rocky path to the clearing and uncovered the two re-buried ostrich egg-wells.

"Dip your tongue in this!" said Mimi, lifting the top off one. The cub didn't need another invitation. He slapped and slurped and splashed with such excitement that the kits got a shower-bath.

"Feeling stronger?" giggled Mimi.

The cub almost managed to say thank you, though it came out as *Nang-oooo…*

"Are you *sure* you're not going to attack us?" ventured Skeema, wondering if this was a trick.

The cub was still very dazed and weak but he managed to whisper, "What d'you take me for? A sneaking snake? A jackal?"

"I trust you," said Mimi. "Come with me, Mimi. Take your time."

Slowly, they led him to where the leg lay in the ashes. He shied away from the fiery smell at first, but they showed him the meat under the black crust and in a flash he got busy with his razor-sharp claws and scraped it clean.

The kits watched him eat, spellbound by his steady concentration and amazed by the noises he made. *Hmmm. Prrrr. Yershhhhh. Glub. Ahhhh.*

He seemed to be sleep-eating. It was only when the bone was licked clean that he gave a sudden twitch that ran through his entire body. And suddenly he was himself again. He ran his rough tongue round his chops and sighed. "Nice," he said, and slowly turned his yellow eyes on Skeema, Mimi and Little Dream.

Chapter 8

For a moment the kits were unable to move. The calm, unblinking stare of his burning eyes drained the strength out of them. The eyes narrowed and the lion cub's wide mouth sprang open like a trap. They braced themselves for the roar that would knock them down like dry leaves. And then he yawned. After that he shook himself noisily.

He suddenly realised how terrified the meerkat kits were. "I'm so sorry!" he said. "I wasn't thinking. You needn't worry about me pouncing on you. Have you never heard the saying – *Feed a cat and he'll be your friend for life?* No? Well it's true – and besides, I gave you my word. Elephants never forget, they say, and lions never break promises."

"We believe you," said Little Dream. "So… friend… we're looking for… someone. And we thought, well, I thought, you might be able to help us find her. Can you tell us what you're doing here?"

"I was running and running," the cub explained as if they were all in the middle of a conversation. "I was with my mama and my four aunts. We hadn't had a kill for … I can't remember. Anyway, we waited at the waterhole… the dry waterhole… nearly dry. My mama said that eland might come for a drink. Or zebra. And she was right. But they smelled us hiding in the grass and they ran. Such a long way, they ran, and so fast. My legs were too small and too weak." He paused to give one of his legs a lick so that the kits would understand. A tear splashed.

"I roared and I roared!" he said. "But they didn't hear me. They were too far ahead. And I must have gone the wrong way… I smelled water and ended up…"

He couldn't say any more, so Skeema said it for him. "So you found a safe place to rest – but you lost your mama. Yes?"

He nodded.

"We're looking for our mama too," said Little Dream. "She's a Wanderer. I heard her calling to me in a dream. And in my dream I saw pawprints across a salt pan and I had to follow them. So when I saw *your* actual pawprints, I just *had* to see what was at the end of them. And it was you."

"When did you lose your mama?" sniffed the cub.

"When I was very little," put in Mimi. "But I still feel bad about it. So don't worry. I'll help you find your mama and that's a promise from Mimi."

"From *us*!" corrected Skeema. "We'll help you find her. All of us."

"That's what I said," said Mimi. "What's your name, by the way?"

"My faraway name is GRRRROOOOAAAAAHHH!" roared the cub, blowing their fur about as he said it. "And my close-up name is Griff," he added less alarmingly. "Which one do you like best?"

All the kits agreed they liked Griff best, so that was that.

It was getting cool. Then, *puff*! The sun blew out like a birthday candle and the Kalahari darktime came down like The Silent Enemy. One moment it was hot; then it rapidly got chilly. The jackals started up. And the screech-owls. The kits moved closer together for warmth and listened while Griff told them about the Land of the Whispering Grasses, where he roamed with his mama and her sisters.

They were fine hunters, he told them, and not even scared of the terrible horns of the buffalo and the wildebeests. When there was nothing to hunt, his aunts took it in turns to feed him their milk. And when they found zebra or buck, they tried to teach him how to be part of a team that could creep and lie patiently and then chase and chase until the creature was weak enough to kill. "I was ashamed because I was too little to help," he said. "But they always invited me to their feasts. And when the jackals sneaked up and knocked me over and stole my portion, they said not to worry. Mama said that if I study hard, one day I will grow big and strong and scatter my enemies with the loudness of my roar. They said that one day I'll be able to outrun them all. But now they're gone. I've lost them. What shall I do?"

"Well, don't worry, you've got us now," said Little Dream.

"I'm sure we can help you find your family, but we meerkats are suntime creatures," explained Skeema, shivering. "We need to rest in the darktime. Which is good because it'll give us time to come up with a proper plan. But it's getting really cold now and if we don't hurry up and find a scrape or a burrow quickly, we shall f-f-freeze."

"It was very kind of you to feed me," whispered the lion cub, lifting his nicely-filled tummy. "Thank you. Now, why don't you squeeze up under the folds of my belly? You'll be snug there, and safe until the sun comes up again?"

The kits couldn't have been snugger. But the lion cub was too full and too exhausted to keep watch. His eyelids drooped and in moments he was sound asleep.

That's why it was no trouble at all for three Blah-blahs to creep up at first light and tangle him in their net.

Shadow saw them come and he saw them go. He did not like what was happening. He could not prevent it, but he was a thoughtful boy and he made a mental note of everything.

Chapter 9

The kits had come across Vroom-vrooms before. Uncle Fearless had taught them that they were mobile escape tunnels. "Special moving burrows, what-what!" he had answered when Mimi had questioned him long ago. "The Blah-blahs don't bother to dig extra passages to escape along in emergencies. So they keep Vroom-vrooms close by to jump into. Then they can get away fast if danger comes."

They also knew how dangerous Vroom-vrooms were, charging along like buffaloes. One had run right over Uncle and Little Dream once, but luckily they had not been touched by its spinners, so they lived to tell the tale.

Why no one heard the Vroom-vroom coming, none of the kits could say. But suddenly there were loud cries: *BLAH-BLAH! BLAH-BLAH-BLAH!*

These were accompanied by frightened snarls, growls, screams, scuffling – and the swish of the net that closed over poor Griff!

Perhaps because they were lighter sleepers than Griff, at least the Really Mads woke up in time to rush for cover. From the hiding place where they lay shaking, the kits watched in horror as the Blah-blahs trussed up Griff until he was as helpless as a fly wrapped tight in a spider's cocoon. There was nothing they could do but watch in horror as he was hoisted up on a pole

between the shoulders of two grim-looking Blah-
blahs and carried away and out of sight. Now
that they were alert and listening hard, they had
no difficulty in hearing the Vroom-vroom roar
into life somewhere on the edge of Green Island.
Then it growled away into the distance across

the almost lifeless desert.

It was still early suntime when, shaking with cold and with no time for a proper, leisurely Warm-up, Skeema, Mimi and Little Dream stood together by the dead fire, feeling miserable and aimless. So far, nobody had come up with any sort of plan.

"Uncle Fearless would know what to do," said Skeema. "And he's a brilliant tracker. I think we should go back to Far Burrow and get his advice. Don't you think so, Mimi? Besides, he's bound to be worried sick about us."

"He's not worried about me," said Mimi bitterly. "All he cares about is that fluffy female."

"Now, that's not fair!" replied Skeema. "He would die for us and you know it!"

"But we promised Griff we would help him find his mama," Little Dream reminded them. "We can't do that if we don't go and rescue him! We just haven't got time to go back to Far Burrow right now. I really think we should follow the Vroom-vroom. You don't need to be clever to follow Vroom-vroom tracks when they're fresh. But the sand will cover them if we don't hurry!"

"Good plan, Dreamie!" said Skeema. "You're right. There's no time to lose. Poor old Griff has had a rough time and besides, it was really friendly of him to keep us warm, don't you think?"

"Yes, and it was pretty special of him not to eat us, too," added Little Dream.

Speaking of eating made the kits hungry and if they were going on a rescue mission they'd need plenty of energy. They sniffed at the dirt, ready to dig for breakfast-bugs. "Look here!" cried Mimi. Close by the ostrich egg-wells, another broad leaf had appeared, folded neatly into a parcel. This time it contained orange fruit, nuts, a paste made of crushed seeds and some fat, wriggling maggots. Just the job for breakfast! The kits tucked in, too hungry to even wonder where it came from.

Suddenly, a ray of sunlight caught the glass beads sewn on to the leather pouch that Mimi had found. Even though he was wearing the Blah-blah eye-protectors he always wore, Little Dream was still dazzled by the way they glittered.

"What's in this?" he asked, picking up the pouch and shaking it. It rattled. He put his paw inside the pouch and pulled out a pawful of beautifully painted pieces of ostrich shell.

"I don't know what these are but, I shall take them with me," announced Little Dream. "You never know – they might come in handy."

"And I shall take this to be my tall stick, like

the one belonging to the shape of the Blah-blah warrior I saw in the cave," announced Skeema. He picked up from the ground the strong, white, hollow bone that came from the shin of an ostrich. He waved it like a spear in one paw while he lifted the Snap-Snap in the other and squeaked it.

Not to be out-done, Mimi grabbed a handful of feathers and porcupine quills and stuck them in her headband. "Now I look important, like

a secretary bird. And I can strut and peck and stamp and look fearsome. And if an enemy comes close, I shall *prick* him like this." In a flash, she snatched a quill and jabbed it in Skeema's bottom.

"Yikes!" he squealed and jabbed her back with his stick.

A giggle made them all stop and bob and listen hard.

"Hyena!" warned Skeema with a shudder. "Stay together!"

He was mistaken about the hyena. It was Shadow who was laughing at the little warrior-meerkats. He had been looking down through a gap in the thorn fence in front of the cave. He put his hand over his mouth to stifle the noise. Even so, he couldn't stop the tears of merriment from pouring down his cheeks.

Chapter 10

It was easy for the Really Mads to find the Vroom-vroom's trail and follow it, and quite honestly, they had not expected to catch up with it so quickly. They had hardly lost sight of Green Island and there it was – stuck in a steep dune with one of its back spinners lying in the soft, hot sand. The Blah-blahs were in a temper.

"*Blah-BLAH-Blah-blah!*" screamed the Chief, the one with the reddest face. The others leaned against the side of the Vroom-vroom and tried to tip it back. *Dammit-grabbit!* One was small with baboon's ears and there was a giant one with a safari hat like Uncle Fearless's, only bigger than a tortoise-shell.

Red-face took the spinner off the back of the Vroom-vroom and staggered around to the front with it, to put it in the space left by the one that had come off.

"Go, go, go!" whispered Skeema, and while the hunters were concentrating on the spinner, the kits skittered around to the back of the Vroom-vroom and peered in. Straight away, they saw Griff, still cruelly bundled up in the net.

When he saw *them*, Griff's sad face brightened. He curled his lip, ready to roar a greeting. Quickly they waved and put their paws over their mouths, meaning, *Shush*! "Lie still," they whispered, saying the words big so Griff could lip-read them. "We can't get you out yet. We'll rescue you later."

"*Blah-BLAH!*" barked Red-face and
started trudging through the sand towards the
back of the Vroom-vroom. The kits dived for
cover underneath while he pulled the door open
and rattled around for something clunky.

"We've got to get inside and go with them,"
hissed Mimi.

"We can't," Skeema hissed back. "The
Blah-blahs will see us. We need to get on top,
somehow. Ah! Look here…!" An untidy bundle,
mostly made up of poles and camping equipment
was tied on to the roof-rack with rope. A piece
of it was dangling down. "Quick, Mimi! Hold
this and give me a leg-up!" urged Skeema. He
passed the Snap-snap and his long bone-stick to
Little Dream. His sister made a kit's-cradle with
her paws and, placing his hind paw in it, he

managed to grab the end of the rope and heave himself up on to the roof. Little Dream tossed him up his weapons and Skeema tucked them away in the folds of the canvas.

"Come on!" he hissed, but quickly realised that there was no way that Mimi or Little Dream could reach the end of the rope. He slid down the rope again, leaving his back legs dangling. Mimi jumped and was able to grab his ankles. Then she let down her tail and Little Dream was able to use that as a rope. The worst part was when he got his sharp

little claws into her body-fur and pulled himself up and over her. "OO-OW! OO!" Next he scrambled up and over his brother – "EEK! OOCH! OUCH!"

"Do you *mind?*" grumbled Skeema, as Little Dream stuck a paw on his unfortunate nose.

"Sorry!" squeaked Little Dream. But at last he was on the roof and able to help haul up the others.

Quickly, they hid themselves in the folds of canvas – and they were only just in time. With a lot of snarls and grunting and sweating, the Blah-blahs fixed the sleeping Vroom-vroom and then woke it up. Awake, it was in an even worse temper than they were. It roared with rage as it heaved itself off the sand dune and on to firmer ground.

"Hang on tight!" warned Mimi. "Grip with your teeth and claws!" The Vroom-vroom grumbled as it began to trot and shouted louder as it started to gallop, bucking and swaying and kicking up dust like a charging rhino. Goodness knows how the terrified kits managed to cling on, but somehow they did.

On and on they rushed, the sights and smells of the Upworld changing around them so quickly that after a while they all began to feel dreadfully sick and dizzy. And when at last the roaring stopped and the Vroom-vroom was still and only ticking in the heat like a weary cicada, they found themselves peeping out at wire fences and big white blocks.

*

Beneath the roof, where the kits clung dizzily to the luggage, the Vroom-vroom cracked open at the sides and the Blah-blahs broke out, like ugly chicks from a square egg.

109

"*Blah-blah! Blah-dammit!*" barked Red-face, the chief. For a moment, as he stretched himself to his full height, his head, with its huge tortoise shell of a helmet, was level with Skeema. He was so close that Skeema could smell his breath. It was nasty and sour, like smoke from a bush fire. At first Skeema considered burrowing deeper into the canvas, but he remembered how he had found the wriggling stone-bug. "Keep still!" he warned himself, and the Blah-blah chief moved on.

Red-face and the others cracked the Vroom-vroom open at the back. No sooner had they done so than Griff let out a hiss like a nest of cobras.

"*Blah-blah! Dammit! Grabbim!*" yelled Red-face. The giant and Baboon-ears tugged at the net and tumbled it on to the ground.

110

Griff could do little more than growl and hiss and show the Blah-blahs what he would do to them if he were free. They pushed the pole through the net again and two of the Blah-blahs lifted him up with it. They grumbled and grunted. *"Uh! Oof! Aha! Grabbim! Dammit!"*

Baboon-ears suddenly gave a scream.

"Good old Griff!" whispered Mimi. "He got his claws into that one!"

"Where are they taking him?" said Little Dream.

"Let's follow and find out," said Skeema. "We'll have to jump for it."

It was a long way down, but jump they all did, breaking their fall by rolling over and over. They had no worries about the Blah-blahs seeing them because they had their paws full with the struggling Griff.

The kits bobbed up and down, trying to attract Griff's attention. At last he caught sight of them, and immediately he calmed down.

"*Blah-blah!*" grunted the giant, obviously thinking that the noises he was making had frightened the spirited little scratcher into silence.

"Don't worry. We're still here!" Skeema mouthed, as they followed silently after them.

Chapter 11

The kits managed to keep out of sight behind the Blah-blahs, who were concentrating on carrying the lion cub. They made their way along a track that ran among cages and small patches of trodden ground, surrounded by shining wire with spikes on it sharper than thorns. In these wired-off areas, dazed creatures stood single and silent and drooping, staring at the sky.

An ostrich gave the meerkats a look and a tut as they passed but then scratched aimlessly at the ground, as if the ground were more

interesting. A porcupine scuttled away and hid in a small box.

"Why are you here?" Little Dream asked a miserable kudu as they passed. But the kudu said nothing.

On they went, past a zebra with a coat as dull as the dust he stood on; an oryx and an eland, rippling their shoulders to scatter the flies that settled on them in clouds. Then a row of bored and circling cats, padding aimlessly around the little spaces they were trapped in – a raggy-looking leopard, a cheetah with a limp, an old Kalahari lion with a tatty grey-black mane.

"Ask the cheetah," suggested Skeema, so Little Dream asked, "Why are you here?" But the cheetah was only interested in his meat – dead meat in a bucket.

"What *is* going on?" Mimi wondered aloud.

The Blah-blahs stopped at an enclosure next to the old lion. They opened the heavy, barred gate and took Griff in, the three of them holding him down as they untangled him from the net. They backed away, expecting him to give them a fight, but the cub was worn out. He lay panting as they retreated and closed the heavy gate behind them.

Baboon-ears tipped some water into a dish and

dropped a rattling handful of something dry into another. Then Red-face led the Blah-blahs away.

*

"Action stations, Wup! Wup!" cried Skeema, as the kits slipped under the wire.

Griff was lying on a mound of earth in front of a small cave that had been dug into it. To get to him, the kits had had to cross a deep ditch. It was no trouble for them to scramble down one side and up the other, but it was too wide for a lion cub to leap across without getting hurt by the dreadful wire. The kits lay down quietly with Griff, not saying anything at first. They just snuggled up to him and let him feel their hearts beating until they were all feeling more settled and sure of themselves.

Then Griff told them what they knew he was feeling. "I don't like it here. I want my Mama.

Why am I here?"

"Ask the Kalahari lion," suggested Skeema.

Griff called out to his neighbour who opened his mouth but could not raise a roar in reply. It was as if his throat was clogged with dust. He flicked his tail, more like a cow-camel than a King of the Plains.

Mimi had made up her mind. "These Blah-blahs are bad," she said. "They are not at all like our Click-clicks at home. They make threat-noises all the time. I think they are another tribe altogether."

"I don't understand," said Griff, so they told him all about the Blah-blahs, and the Click-click tribe back home, with their funny pointy mounds and their eye-protectors and their Vroom-vrooms.

"But if these Blah-blahs are not Click-clicks,

what tribe are they?" asked Griff.

"I think they must be the Dammit-Grabbim tribe," said Mimi. "And I think I know why they brought you here."

"You do?" cried Skeema. "Why then?"

"Because it's the dry season!" said Mimi.

"What's that got to do with it?" asked Little Dream.

"Well, you can see how big and fat they are," said Mimi, and the others agreed. "So they must eat a lot. And when food is scarce near their burrow, they go out in their Vroom-vrooms and capture any animals they can. Then they bring them here so they can eat them whenever they feel hungry."

"Mimi! I had no idea you were so clever!" said Skeema.

"Nor does anybody else!" grumbled Mimi,

getting huffy. "*Including* Uncle. If he did, he wouldn't go off looking for other princesses to join the Really Mads."

"But it was only one, and I'm sure she's very nice, really," Skeema reminded her.

"Yes, but she's not much use, is she?"

Griff interrupted them. He was horrified. "Hey! I don't want to get eaten!" he said. "Don't let them eat me!"

"We won't," said Little Dream, giving him a comforting pat. "Skeema will come up with a plan. He's good at them."

And sure enough, Skeema did come up with a plan. "We shall wait till darktime," he mused, "until the Blah-blahs are asleep – and then we shall all run away together. And then we'll go and look for your mama."

"And our mama," put in Little Dream.

"*And* our mama," agreed Skeema. "We'll find Griff's mama first and then we shall have a jolly good search for ours. OK, Dreamie?"

"But I can't get across the ditch!" said Griff anxiously. "My legs are too small and too weak. And I can't get through the wire."

"Ah, but there's no need to go *through* it," said Skeema with a crafty grin, "when we've got these." And he held up his front paws, each with four sharp claws – perfect for digging.

Chapter 12

When the sun fell out of the sky, the kits peeped out from Griff's little dug-out cave and were surprised to find that there was still so much light. Since their darktimes were normally spent in a chamber, deep under the earth, they didn't know about the moon and the stars.

All night the meerkats had dug fast and deep but they had never tried digging a tunnel wide enough for a lion cub to get through before. It was cruel work. Though it was the darktime, the air was hot and full of electricity that lifted their

121

fur into crackling points. Black thunder-clouds
slid across the moon and hid it.

"Shoulder-to-shoulder," puffed Skeema.
"Maybe that will do the trick!"

Sadly it didn't. They were used to working one
in front of the other to clear out burrows. Being
side-by-side meant getting in one another's way.

Griff did his best to help, but he kept getting
in the way too. And besides, his claws were the

wrong shape for tunnelling. He could scoop
– a bit like a puppy – but he was no good at
tunnelling.

Bit by bit, they all began to tire. Not
surprisingly, since he wasn't used to digging,
Griff was soon flat on his tummy, gasping for
breath.

"This is not going to work," said Mimi when
she too collapsed.

Even Skeema, who was normally one to look
on the bright side, began to have doubts. "It's not
so much the length of the tunnel," he admitted
between gasps. "The problem is shifting all the
loose sand out of the way."

"Let's just keep at it till we drop," said Little
Dream bravely.

"I just… can't… go on," puffed Mimi,
collapsing again. "What's going to happen to

me?" she wailed. She could hardly stop herself from bursting into tears. "I'm never going to make it!"

"NEVER SAY NEVER!" boomed an echoing voice. "Tunnel hard, tunnel true, and you never know *what* you'll dig up, what-what!"

"UNCLE FEARLESS!" squealed the kits.

"Reinforcements!" cried Uncle. "Well, not exactly an army, but two willing supporters nonetheless!" he went on, popping out of the tunnel and giving himself a shake-up. "Radiant and I heard you working and dug down ourselves from the other side of the wire to join up with you!"

He suddenly noticed Griff towering over him. "WUP-WUP! DIVE DIVE DIVE!" he yelled and threw himself back down the entrance to the tunnel.

"Wait! This is Griff!" called Little Dream.

"He's our friend!"

"Grrr-owwww do you do?" growled Griff.

Uncle popped his head out again. He still didn't look too confident.

"Who's *we?*" said Mimi, astonished. "You said there were two of you…"

"Are you sure we're safe with … *you-know-who?*" asked Uncle.

Griff raised a paw and solemnly swore that he would never harm any meerkat.

Uncle turned and called down into the tunnel behind him, "All's well, Radiant! The kits are here. Everyone's alive and scratching, by all that's crunchy-crawly! Come on through!"

Radiant appeared.

"Bless her!" said Uncle, tipping his head. Then, turning to Mimi he said, "You know, I'd never have got here without her!"

Radiant shook the dust
of her fabulous fur
and said shyly,
"Hello, chaps!"
Then it was
her turn to catch
sight of Griff for
the first time. She
ducked out
of sight
again,

sharpish. Mimi looked at Uncle, turned, then
chased down the tunnel after Radiant.

"Oh dear…" said Uncle Fearless, fearing the
worst. "I was rather hoping that Mimi would
have got over her jealousy by now." But a
moment later, his two princesses popped out of
the tunnel again, not arguing at all. "I know he

looks fierce, but he's very gentle really," Mimi said, steering Radiant into the open again. "He made us a promise not to harm us and we've promised to help him find his mother. Only we need to tunnel him out of here, and we haven't got the strength for it."

"Then… if I'm not intruding… perhaps I can lend a paw?" said Radiant hesitantly. "How do you feel about that?"

"Oh, all right," said Mimi trying not to sound too keen. She scraped awkwardly at the sand with her paw.

"I think what Mimi means," said Skeema with a grin, "is that apart from Uncle, she's never been happier to see anyone in her life! Right, Mimi?"

"You arrived just in the nick of time!" added Little Dream. "We'd just begun to think we'd never manage to get Griff out of here."

"Jolly unusual, isn't it?" said Radiant. "Rescuing a *lion*, I mean?"

"He's lost his Mama too, like us, and we're helping him find her," said Skeema. "We'll explain later. Right now, we need all claws to the sand!"

There was *just* time for a quick celebration, naturally. What meerkat could miss out on a bit of squealing and cuddling and rolling and play-nipping at a time like this? ... and yes... a bit of a squirt all round from Uncle. "Good show!" he cried. "All together again, at last!"

Griff looked on, feeling a bit left out. "What about me?" he said sadly. "Don't I get a squirt?"

"Certainly!" cried Uncle and obliged him with an extra-large one. "There! Now you can call yourself an honorary member of the Really Mad Mob! So come on! Let's get widening!"

"One last thing... You still haven't told us

128

how in the Upworld you found us!" Skeema said.

"Aha!" said Uncle, with a starlit twinkle in his one good eye. "I thought you might ask that! Well, the answer, my boy, lies in my helmet! Hold out your paws, Little Dream!" He removed his hat with a flourish and tipped into his paws a heap of little painted shell-fragments, all the colours of the rainbow. "Someone dropped these, I believe?" he added.

"That was me!" said Little Dream eagerly. "I found them in a little pouch at Green Island. I *knew* they'd come in handy! I thought if you came looking for us you'd easily see the colours, so I decided to drop one every time we passed an ostrich or a tortoise or a tsamma melon bush, just in case you were on our trail."

"Plus you added a nice little squirt to each bit of shell, eh laddy? Bravo, my boy! All we had to do was follow our noses, by all that's wet and whiffs! That special spicy Really Mad aroma is as good as any signpost!"

Suddenly the lights blazed on in the big white block and there were sounds of Blah-blahs making a fuss. A shocking bright flash-light came dancing along the track among the animal enclosures. It reached out, lighting up gates, throwing long, frightening shadows, making the eyes of startled cats glimmer like the twinkling lights in the sky.

"Down!" warned Skeema, for he had heard the clumping footsteps and caught the sweaty smell of the giant Blah-blah with the safari hat as big as a tortoise shell. It was he who was holding the light and waving it around like a fizz-fire. He had arrived at the gate of Griff's enclosure and was rattling it hard. The noise was terrifying. RATTLE-CLANG-BANG-CLANG!

Griff began to tremble but he did his best to be brave. He got his growl going and stood as tall as he could on all fours. "He's coming to eat me," he told the kits. "But I'm not going to give in without a fight! In the loudest voice he could muster he shouted his far-off name – "ROOOOAAAARRRRRGH!"

The Blah-blah shouted something back. *Sherr-dup! Sherr-dup- dammit!*" and waved the light at him.

Mimi had had enough. "We're not scared of you!" she yelled.

She ducked through the bars of the gate and ran straight at him. When the giant jumped back in shock, she started high-stepping round him

in dizzying circles, nodding her head-feathers
wildly like a secretary-bird on the attack. When
she was certain that the Blah-blah was properly
confused and alarmed, she let out a squawk and
stamped on his toe. He hardly felt it, but he had
never seen a sight like Mimi in his life. What
was it? Some sort of porcupine? A bird? … a
porcubird? It made him very nervous. He bent
down to swat the pesky thing away.

This gave Skeema the perfect chance to let him have it in the backside with the sharp end of his long stick. *AAAH-YEEE!* The Blah-blah trumpeted like an elephant and ran for his life.

"Played, Skeema!" said Mimi. "High four!" And they clashed claws.

"Well done, kits! Right, sharp, now!" said Uncle. "We've got to get out of here! Before they come back, what-what!" And with that, they got their heads down and dug for all they were worth.

*

The meerkats dug and dug for what felt like several darktimes, but though they were tired, they kept going, encouraging one another, sensing that slowly but surely they were making progress.

Mimi couldn't help marvelling at the work

133

Radiant put in. "Maybe she's not *completely* useless," she thought to herself. Then, with a little sideways glance at her fellow princess, she redoubled her efforts. And when Radiant gave her an approving smile, she felt a rush of pride.

With all claws to the sand, as Skeema had put it, it wasn't long before the tunnel was wide enough even for Griff to crawl through.

Soon, the escape-party had managed to dig under the ditch and under the wire and on to the drive leading up to the main gate in double-quick time. The gate was no problem for The Really Mads. They shot through the bars as easily as ants up a creeper. "Free at last!" yelled Little Dream, squealing with the pleasure of it. "Come on, Griffy!"

But Griff just watched in terror. Was he strong enough to leap over those terrible spikes?

Trembling, he looked up at the gate.

Suddenly, there was a sound of doors slamming and the Vroom-vroom gave a roar behind him. Its piercingly bright lights lit up the drive and made Griff's terrified eyes shine like two yellow moons. His heart thudded. *My legs were too small and weak to keep up with Mama*, he thought. *And now I shall get left behind forever.*

"Take a run at it!" screamed the Really Mads. "Jump, Griffy! You can do it!"

But it was Radiant who realised that what Griff really needed at this moment was a little motherly encouragement. "You know what your mama would say?" she called quietly through the gate. "She'd say: *You're a big cub now, Griff. You know you've got what it takes. Just trust yourself.*"

The Vroom-vroom staggered forward. There

were cries of *Grabbim-Dammit!* from the furious Blah-blahs.

But Griff *was* a big cub now, and he put a spurt on. "GRRRRAAHHHH!" he roared and soared like an eagle.

He cleared the spikes by no more than a whisker. But he cleared them and that was all that mattered.

"Majestic!" cried Uncle. "Now – run like the wind!" Secretly, he feared that the Vroom-vroom would be upon them before they could find a bolt hole on the great open plain with only a single tree in sight.

But Uncle Fearless need not have worried. All four of it's spinners were punctured!

Hidden behind that single tree, and darker than the shadow that hid him, a boy was watching, and he was happy to see the wild things run free.

He ran his thumb over the point of his spear and clicked his tongue in satisfaction. He was pleased with the sharpness of his tyre-buster.

Flattening his tight curls with his hand, he felt sparks snapping at his fingers. *Storm coming*, he thought and wrapped his eland-skin cloak tightly about him. *The Great Thirst is over*.

Chapter 13

Griff and the Really Mads had reached the edge of a ravine lined by stunted shrubs and whispering grasses before they dared stop for breath. The ground was all broken and churned up by the hooves of animals hoping – at the fly-bitten end of this this dry season – to find even a puddle to lick. Uncle sniffed and thought he could feel the weight of heavy clouds over his head.

"Careful now," he panted. "I'll go ahead and take a look at what's down there." He was nervous. The darktime is not a time for meerkats to range about in the Upworld. And right now they were in very dark, very strange territory, where enemies crept and crawled.

The earth began to tremble. For a flickering moment, the sky split and lit up like suntime. Blinding bolts of lightning hissed and stabbed at the sands, throwing up the silhouettes of a line of elephants coming towards them. They were desperate for water and the great bulls were flapping their ears and swinging their tusks and trunks in a rage. Another flash. "Fizz-fire!" cried Uncle. "Those tuskers won't have to wait long for a drink and a mudbath. The rains are here!"

The elephants began to trot forward like a dark line of moving hills, each one holding the tail of the one in front with his trunk. To the meerkats, even the baby elephants looked like mountains of flesh.

"Cover your ears!" yelled Uncle. It was good advice. The fizz-fire was quickly followed by a sky-crash louder than the hooves of ten thousand migrating wildebeests. It scared even the mighty elephants, so that they screamed and trumpeted – and suddenly – it was a stampede!

"Down! Before they trample us flat! Down into the ravine!" cried Uncle and led everyone down the steep slope.

Even in their panic, the great beasts were anxious to keep to the higher ground. When they realised that the land was dropping away sharply, they reared and turned, then dashed sideways, following the line of parched shrubs. Even so, their great flat feet loosened earth and rocks from the edge of the gully and sent them crashing down.

"Avalanche!" screamed Mimi as she tumbled

into the dip. She saw Little Dream go rolling past her down the bank, like a curled-up beetle. Then, by the dazzling light of another zig-zag of fizz-fire, she caught a glimpse of Uncle and Radiant tumbling together. A huge rock bounced over her and narrowly missed Griff and Skeema, who were just ahead of her.

All too soon, Mimi lay stunned and scared to death at the bottom of the gully. The noise and the darkness and the crashing earth and rocks spread over her like the dreaded shadow of The Silent Enemy.

There was no sign of her little mob or of poor Griff. She had never felt more alone.

The rain began to come down, at first in fat drops that thudded on to her head and back and pounded into the thirsty sand. Then it came down in lumps, then like a waterfall. Then it felt as if all the air had disappeared and had been replaced by water. She tucked her head under the arch of her little body and made a space to breathe.

"Yip-yip! To me! All in to me!" It was Uncle, sounding his rallying-call in the darkness.

Somehow Mimi pulled herself together and scrambled towards the sound. By the light of a fizz-flash, she spied Radiant dragging Little Dream out by the scruff of his neck from under a tangle of sand and broken branches and stones. And there, a little further along the gully Uncle stood tall, calling, calling…

"Where's Griff?" yelled Mimi. "Is he all right? Has anyone seen him?"

Before anyone could answer, there was a gurgling sound and then a rushing *swoosh*! of water racing towards them. "What is it, Uncle?" cried Skeema.

"Oh no! By all that sweeps and swirls! This must be a dry riverbed we're in!" called Uncle. "And if I'm not mistaken, the river wants its bed back, right now! Brace yourselves, everyone, and cling together!"

"But Fearless!" came the nervous voice of Radiant. "My dear, I'm not sure whether I can swim!"

"Me neither, my Fluff!" cried Uncle. "But hang on to my fur! We're just about to find out!"

"Help!" wailed the kits in one voice.

The first wave struck them like a wall and

swept them along as if they were no heavier than dry leaves.

*

Luckily, as Shadow was just able to observe from the bank of the new-born river, meerkats *can* swim if they have to. They were lit up for him by a purple sheet of lightning, hung down from the swollen, shifting clouds. He grunted with satisfaction and then lost sight of the meerkat mob as they floated round the bend.

Un-luckily, meerkats are not built to keep swimming for long.

The Really Mads struggled bravely to keep together without dragging one another down. They managed to steer clear of some nasty-looking rocks and then they came to a waterfall.

It was then that they discovered they were not
the only creatures to be swept away.

First, they bounced off a springbok. That was

all right. He wasn't too hard.

Then they sailed past a small fleet of snorting warthogs that had no trouble at all sailing along.

Some zebras struggled in a line to get across from one bank to the other, nodding and kicking the water under them, snuffling and blowing raspberries.

"Look out!" yelled Little Dream. "Snake!"

It wasn't a snake that any of them had seen before, but it was huge and fat and winding rapidly towards them. "Stand by to repel boarders!" commanded Uncle. Mimi felt for her headband. The feathers in it had been swept away, but a couple of porcupine prickles remained.

Skeema braced himself. "Wait! He's coming on my side. Hold my sharp stick!" he said to Mimi and she managed to take it without letting

go of her grip on Uncle's fur. That left Skeema in
a position to hang on too, and at the same time
to dip the Snap-snap under the water and give
him a hard squeeze. The hungry snake swung
closer. "Come on, come on…" said Skeema
through gritted teeth. "Show me where you
shine!"

He didn't have long to wait. A jagged fizz-
fire flash lit up the reptile's head. Before it had
time to open its jaws and swallow Skeema –
PPPSSSSSSS! – the Snap-snap spat a fast jet of
muddy water right in the snake's beady eye!

That did it. The side-winding brute beat a fast retreat.

"Shot, sir!" said Uncle, though not with a great deal of energy. "Where did you learn that trick?"

"I got it off an oogpister beetle," said Skeema, though he hardly had the puff to speak. Like the others, he felt his fur getting waterlogged. He was sinking fast.

"I can't hold on to you much longer, Fearless," gasped Radiant. "Perhaps it would be better if I drifted away. Then you can save your strength for the kits…"

"Don't give up, my dear!" urged Fearless. "Hang on. And everyone, kick! Kick for that yellow rock!"

Kick as they might, the brave Really Mads had not the strength to swim much further.

They closed their eyes. There was nothing they could do but let the wild young river take them where it wanted.

Chapter 14

When it saw that the meerkats were too tired to swim to *it*, the yellow rock couldn't help thinking: "I wonder if it would help if I went over to *them*…"

It paddled itself alongside them and noticed that they all had their eyes closed.

"ROOOAAAARGHH! ALL ABOARD!" roared the rock. Only of course, it wasn't really a yellow rock.

"Chins up, everyone! Paddle over to me. In-out, in-out! That's it. You're doing really well…"

It was Griff, moving about on the surface as confidently as any turtle. The Really Mads heard the confidence in his cheery voice and they discovered that they weren't doomed after all. "Keep going! That's it! Grab my coat!" he urged.

And his invitation did the trick. The eyes of all the meerkats flew open and they started thinking about living again.

"Heave!" cried Uncle as he hauled his sodden body on to the cub's strong back. "Remind me to lose a bit of weight, what-what!" he joked, slapping his fat tum. "Now give me your paws, everyone."

Slowly, painfully, one by one, the kits were heaved out of the river and on to Griff's back.

"This is fun, don't you think?" Griff remarked as he headed for the riverbank. "I like doing this new thing…"

"It's called swimming," puffed Little Dream
helpfully.

"Is it?" said Griff, paddling along very nicely.
"Well, I like swimming. I've got just the paws for
it, don't you think?"

"Jolly good show!" said Uncle. "Fine work, laddy. Now, would you mind awfully getting us on to dry land. Some of us are feeling a little…"

Little Dream finished the sentence for him. "…weak," he said. He wasn't ashamed to admit it and he added, "our legs are too small and too weak for this kind of work."

"Really?" said Griff, suddenly looking rather pleased with himself. "And there was me worrying that it was only *my* legs that felt that way!"

*

When a honey badger is chased by its enemies, it lets out a stink filthy enough to put off even the hungriest jackal or hyena. There were the remains of such a whiff in the earth-hole or scrape, high above the flowing water where Griff was resting peacefully that darktime. He didn't mind; he was happy just to be out of the rain. And besides, the honey-badger was delicious. He licked his lips.

The Really Mads excused themselves from curling up with Griff. They preferred to gather the last of their strength to dig a hole for themselves… a little downwind.

They had never slept more soundly and they woke, refreshed, to the cry of excited birds and the clap and clatter of storks's bills. When they climbed back into the Upworld again, the clouds had gone, the sun was out, and they were able to look down at the feasting crowds. Along with dazzlingly white egrets and dancing cranes, the storks dipped for frogs and tiger-fish and all sorts of new life that wriggled in the wonderful new brown water.

The meerkats didn't have far to look for their

own breakfast once their tummy-pads were warm. Indeed, breakfast pretty well walked into their open jaws. The moist sand close by attracted countless skinks and lizards and beetles and termites and scorpions, all just under the surface of the sand.

Little Dream had work to do. He took his turn to be on watch in the top branches of a camelthorn tree, but even he didn't go hungry. There were tender new buds to nibble and one or two yellow flowers, and while he lifted his head to keep an eye on a pair of somersaulting bataleur eagles overhead, he was able to snack on sweet new-hatched moths and winged bugs, drifting by on the breeze.

"Wup-wup, the group! Let's go! Far Burrow is calling!" called Uncle cheerily. "But first we have a promise to keep to Griff, what-what! He would like to be reunited with his mama, I believe."

"And I should like to be reunited with mine," Little Dream reminded him. *Reunited* was just the word he was looking for.

"Harrrumph! Yes, well… We'll have to see what we can do, eh, Dreamie?" said Uncle, trying to sound more hopeful than he was. "Right, then. Is everybody set for the off?"

"Ready!" came the answer in chorus.

"Then hoist up your tummies!"

"Like this, Griff!" laughed the kits and they showed him. "One-two-three… HUP!"

And with that, they set off, following the river which Uncle was sure was one of the waterways that fed the salt pans after a good rain. Already the yellow grasses were turning green and pinkish flowers had sprung out of the branches of the soap-bushes. In the distance, ostriches

boomed, zebras whinnied, and buck leaped for joy. All around, grasshoppers and cicadas urged them on with their rasping and ticking. *Kee-pup! Kee-pup! Kee-pup!* Giraffes poked their elegant necks among distant trees, seeking the topmost and tenderest shoots. When they heard the jackals bark, the meerkats stopped in their tracks – but then they saw that Griff was not afraid, so they took courage and pressed forward.

Chapter 15

They left the banks of Wild River and followed the line of another that was calmer and had spilled into small lakes. Skeema looked carefully at one of the pools where lilies were already blooming, surprised to see no other sign of life. Then, with a whirring sound, the dark water itself seemed to lift into the air! Just as quickly, it shattered into a whirring flock of tubby birds that flashed off in all directions.

"Where are they off to in such a hurry, Uncle?" gasped Mimi.

"Ah, dashed clever birds, your sand-grouse!" said Uncle. "They hatch their chicks in the driest part of the desert. So what do they do? They use their breast-feathers like sponges to soak up water and fly it in to them."

"Brilliant!" agreed Skeema. "And when they keep still, you can't even see them! What a trick!"

"Like Mama and my aunts," sighed Griff. "They are the colour of the grasses and the drie-doring shrub. You can look and look and you will not see them. But when they show themselves, they are beautiful and terrible. They are called the Five Beauties."

Radiant gave a start and broke in. "Five, did you say?"

"Mama has four sisters," explained Griff.

"Then, bless me if I didn't see them once,

from far off – long ago when I began my life as a Wanderer!"

"Where?" said Little Dream.

"I was hungry," explained Radiant, "and was searching for damp ground, hoping to surprise a few lizards or blind-worms. I stumbled across a water-hole where the trees grow upside down. The sun had drunk the water and left only a great marsh with a puddle in the middle. It was guarded by crocodiles and hippos. And when an old haartebeest came down to the water to drink, the lionesses sprang out of the grass to catch it. But the hippos gave them away. They opened their great mouths as hippos will and shouted: "Look out! Look out! Five Beauties about!" So the crocodiles rushed the hartebeeste and caught it by the nose. That time the lionesses went as hungry as me."

Griff did his best to turn a whimper into a cough, but he couldn't quite manage it.

"Chin up!" cried Uncle. "Upside down trees you say, Radiant? Baobobs, by all that's strange and carrot-like! I know that water hole. It's full of crocs and hippos all right! This way! Tally-ho! Follow me!"

*

It was almost darktime when the searchers reached Hippo Hole. There was a big moon in the sky and another one in the water. After the rain the water-hole was full to the brim. It was easy to see even from a distance that the muddy margins of the pool were pitted with pawprints and hoofprints of every kind. Every desert-dweller within galloping distance must have turned up to quench its terrible thirst. Most of them were hiding somewhere in the grove of boabob trees. Little gangs of them were waiting their turn to dash through the tall reeds to splash and guzzle some glorious, cool, fresh water. They hoped by turning up in numbers to frighten or outrun enemies planning to feast on them.

Uncle and his search-party were lying low on a boulder far enough away to give them a good safe view of things. Even from there, above the whirring of the crickets and cicadas, they could hear the mad laughter of hyenas. But there was no sign or sound of any big cats.

Griff was whimpering with excitement, his tail sweeping nervously as if he were about to pounce. His yellow eyes scanned the grasses and shrubs for signs of his mother and aunts.

Some elephants sauntered out of the darkness at their ease and dipped in their trunks. Taking their time, they began tossing water casually

over their shoulders. Made bold by this, a crowd of kudu suddenly appeared at the water's edge, the females darting nervously. The big bull whirled round and reared up. He dipped his twisted horns and raised them again with a bellow that was meant as a challenge to any lurking enemy.

His high-pitched fanfare was answered, if very faintly, by a throaty roar.

"Mama?" called Griff, leaping up, all the bristles on his yellow coat standing on end as if he had been struck by fizz-fire. "Mama! I'm here! Can you hear me? Mama!"

"Steady on, Griff, dear boy!" said Uncle. "I heard that roar myself, but it came from a fair way away, wouldn't you say? Can you be absolutely sure it was your mother calling?" Griff didn't stop to answer. He was off at the gallop, racing around the edge of the water-hole, kicking up great gobbets of wet mud. He was heading for the far side where a forest of papyrus reeds grew tall and thick.

"Stay together to stay alive!" warned Uncle, but Griff was far too excited to listen.

"We must head him off!" barked Uncle. "Before it's too late!" He was aware, as Griff was not, of a great danger. At the sound of the disturbance made by his pounding paws in the water, half a dozen scaly monsters slid across the

soupy mud, lowered their snouts, and torpedoed towards him.

"Crocodiles!" Uncle yelled and was off like the wind. "Follow me, the Really Mads, and keep in a straight line, till we catch up with him!"

Radiant and the kits obeyed his order without question. As usual, wise old Fearless knew what he was up to. Griff's puppy-legs were bending and lolloping all over the place in his excitement. As a result, though it was hard work chasing through the gloopy mud and the shallow water, the meerkats were alongside him in no time.

"Steer him up on to the bank!" yelled Uncle and the Really Mads did just that, nipping and nudging at Griff's legs until they all drifted out of the shallows and were high and dry among tussocks of grass on the shore. The crocodiles skimmed to a stop and lowered their ugly snouts, bubbling with disappointment.

He didn't thank them. In fact, Griff was so intent on finding his mama that he hardly seemed to notice that the meerkats were with him. And it was not until he had pushed to the edge of the forest of tall papyrus reeds that he threw himself down on his belly and the others lay with him. In several places the reeds had been parted by the shoulders of eager, lumbering water-seekers. Eyes darting, ears pricked for the slightest sound, the lion cub and the meerkats watched these green alleyways and waited.

Unfortunately, they were not ready for the speed and cunning of the brutes that sprang at them, hard and low, from where the reeds grew thickest. The only warning they had was a hot stink and Uncle's voice bellowing…

"Jackals!"

Chapter 16

There were two of them, a male and a female black-back. They weren't as big and ugly as hyenas and not so round-shouldered – but they were deadly. They had pointy, foxy faces and tall, sensitive ears that swivelled and homed in on the slightest sound. Like leopards, their slender legs were built for speed.

"Supper at last!" they announced and moved in towards the meerkats, grinning. Uncle rolled the kits under his body to protect them and Radiant stood beside him, snarling, puffing out her gorgeous fur. Then, in a move designed to terrify them, the jackals suddenly bounced upwards on all-fours, and landed one on each side of them.

Without warning, Griff bristled and leapt between the attackers, showing them his sharp little teeth and claws. "There's all this big game about, and you decide to hunt little meerkats?" he growled scornfully.

"What's it got to do with you?" growled the male.

"These are my friends," answered Griff. "Leave them alone."

"Or else what?" snapped the female.

"Or else you'll have to fight me."

"Listen, puss!" sneered the male jackal. "Don't try to bite off more than you can chew. Just get out of the way."

"I'm not moving," Griff said calmly.

"That's the spirit, Griff, old boy!" called Uncle. His voice was full of admiration, but there was worry in it too. Each of the jackals was bigger than Griff, and with one on each side, there was no telling which one would strike first.

The female darted at the cub suddenly, snapping at his paw and then pulling back out of reach. Griff stood his ground and snapped back at her. "Run for your lives, meerkats!" he cried. "I can manage these two!" As he spoke, the male closed in from the other side and nipped the opposite leg.

Skeema couldn't help being secretly impressed by the way they operated. *They must have had lots of battle-practice*, he thought. He wondered what Uncle's next move would be and sensed the tension in him as he stood on guard, steady as a rock. The bug disguised as a stone slipped back into Skeema's mind. *I get it*, he thought. *Keep still. No sudden moves.*

That wasn't the way Radiant was thinking, though.

With an athletic bound, she leaped in front of Griff and stretched herself to her full height. "Cowards!" she shouted. "Two against one! Where's the honour in that?"

"I always enjoy my supper with a bit of sauce!" snarled the female, licking her lips. "But your impudence won't save you and nor will a weak little lion cub." Her teeth were surprisingly long and jagged. "Save your breath and take what's coming to you!"

"You can have me if you let the kits go!" cried Radiant. But suddenly Mimi was standing by her side.

"Thank you, but I'm not going anywhere, not me, not me! I'm armed and dangerous!" And she made a thrusting motion with one of her porcupine quills, "Take that!"

No sooner had the eyes of the jackals turned to her than Skeema got behind them and gave the Snap-snap a mighty SQUEAK! that made them jump and spin. That gave Mimi a chance to jab the female in the leg.

But the female was quick and strong and hungry. With a swipe of her paw she disarmed Mimi, knocking her down and pinning her to the ground.

"Leave her alone!" screamed Radiant and flew at her.

"Freeze!" warned the female, lashing out, "or I'll snap her head off."

"You can't scare me! Not Mimi! I'm a

princess!" screamed Mimi defiantly, looking her enemy right in the face.

"Hey! I recognise you!" said the female. "You gave us the slip once before, if I'm not mistaken? You're a Sharpeyes-princess, aren't you? We caught up with you wandering about all on your own, I remember. Close by Red Ebony Point it was, where the weaver birds drive you mad with their chit-chat. Then you kicked sand in my husband's eyes and escaped! Well mark my words, you won't get away with that trick twice!"

Suddenly Little Dream went a bit crazy! He grabbed the female's tail and yanked it. "What Sharpeyes-princess are you talking about? When did you see her? Where was she?"

"Dreamie!" called Uncle, trying to keep his voice steady. "Keep out of the way, there's a good chap."

"Don't you understand, Uncle?" cried Little Dream. "She thought Mimi was Mama!"

Griff seized his chance and lunged at the male, only to be sent sprawling by him.

"Tally-ho!" cried Uncle Fearless, launching himself at the brute and sinking his teeth into his flank. At the same time Skeema poked at him with his pointed stick and was thrilled to hear the jackal shriek with pain.

But the jackal was too strong for them. He shrugged the meerkats aside and rolled Griff over, giving him a couple of nasty bites on the shoulder and finally gripping him round the throat.

"You haven't got a chance of saving these sand-rats!" scoffed the female. "Give up now before you get choked!" Griff struggled bravely, but the jaws at his throat were squeezing the breath out of him.

"Now say goodnight to your princesses…
Uncle!" the female whined in triumph, having
finally pinned down both Mimi and Radiant
with her strong paws.

Suddenly there was a dreadful,
deafening roar like the sky-crash
of a summer storm.

"ROOAAAAAGH!"

"Mama!" shouted Griff as his mother, rippling with muscle and furiously angry, sprang from the forest of reeds and sent the jackals screaming into the darkness.

"There you are, at last!" thundered the fearsome creature, lifting him by the scruff of his neck and shaking him. "Where have you *been* my naughty, lovely boy?"

"It's a long story," laughed Griff, thrilled to be roughed up by her, purring as he felt her rough tongue licking his wounds. "But Mama, I want you to meet…"

At that moment, the other four of the Five Beauties crashed through the papyrus into the open.

Now THAT was scary.

"Great to m-meet you all, I'm sure," stammered Uncle, beating a hasty retreat and pushing

Radiant along ahead of him. "Sorry to have to rush off."

As Uncle and Radiant scampered away, the three meerkat kits turned to say a tearful goodbye to their friend. The unlikely little mob exchanged group licks and rubs and then it was time to go.

"Thanks for saving us, Griffy!" said Mimi. "Don't forget that you're an honorary meerkat now, so come and visit us some time at Far Burrow! You were brilliant! "

"You put up a heck of a fight!" agreed Skeema and for the benefit of Griff's fearsome Mama, he added, "he's terribly brave, you know! See you soon Griff."

"Sorry we can't stay!" sniffed Little Dream. "We've got to find *our* Mama now. Happy hunting and do visit us, won't you!"

"I'm an honor – roary meerkat!" rumbled Griff. "Of course I'd like to see Far Burrow!" He turned to his mother and added hastily. "If Mama doesn't mind."

She dipped her great head under him and nuzzled him and rolled him over to remind him what a young scamp he was. It was clear that she didn't plan to let him go again just yet, but she didn't say no, so that was something.

Uncle and Radiant had stopped at a safe distance and were calling anxiously. So, a little reluctantly, the kits turned and raced after them.

And thus began the long journey home.

*

As Uncle Fearless said later when they had put some distant between themselves and the Five Beauties, "Did you *have* to mention hunting, Dreamie, in front of five hungry lionesses?

178

Whew! Well I hope they didn't think us rude. I mean, manners are manners, and all that! But Radiant and I didn't think that was the ideal moment to wait around to be introduced to them, what-what!"

Chapter 17

The Really Mad mob was almost home at Far Burrow. They had just stopped off at Green Island on the way, as the kits were keen to show its secrets to Uncle and Radiant.

"Remarkable, what-what!" agreed Uncle. They cooled their tongues in the ostrich egg-wells and were surprised and delighted to find enough food for everyone folded up in broad green leaves, laid out on the ground nearby. There were kicking beetles, spiders, some centipedes, a knot of worms, some jumpy crickets and a bunch of roots. It was not the Meerkat Way to wonder how the food had got there. For Shadow, up in his watching-tree, the pleasure of seeing them tucking in was all the thanks he wanted.

"The sound of a lioness in a temper is louder than sky-crash," Radiant said by way of conversation as they chewed things over. "But *five* of them! Gosh! I've had a few shocks in my time, but never anything like that!"

She was surprised to find that Mimi had nuzzled up to her and was running her paws through her fur, tenderly searching out fleas. "I just thought I'd say," said Mimi, clearing her throat with a little nervous cough, "that I think you've been… you know… and it was awfully brave of you to…"

"Oh gosh! Stop!" cried Radiant.

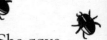

"You'll have me blubbing in a minute!" She gave Mimi a lick and a squeeze. "Lucky I'm not the blubbing sort, eh? I'm just proud and happy to be part of the mob. And I do hope you're happy to have me. Are you?"

"I…" stammered Mimi.

"WE!" chorused the others. "WE're all glad WE've got you!"

Mimi was lost for words. So she took off her head-dress and placed it on Radiant's head. "You have it. It suits you…" she managed to whisper.

Uncle was as happy as a barking gecko to see that they had become firm friends, and just to prove it, he dashed about and gave them all a good, loving squirt.

"I'm glad Griff found his mama," said Skeema.

"I wish we'd found ours," said Little

182

Dream, sadly. "Pity we never got the chance to ask the jackals where they saw her."

"If it *was* dear Fragrant, Dreamie," cautioned Uncle, mildly.

"Well, that dreadful she-jackal mistook Mimi for her, whoever she was," said Radiant. "So the question is, *does* Mimi look anything like her mama?"

"Well, now that you mention it, I must admit, she's the spitting image of her," Uncle said, nodding.

"Then it *must* be Mama they saw!" said Little Dream, eyes wide and sparkly. "And one day we shall find her, I'm sure of it."

"Hurrumph," said Uncle. "That's the stuff, Dreamie! Never say never, what-what!"

"I wonder…" said Little Dream, jumping up and running towards the path that led up to the cave.

"Wait for me, for me!" wailed Mimi as she chased after him, racing Skeema up the path.

"What now, kits?" puffed Uncle, following them into the echoing chamber, Radiant at his side.

When his eyes got used to the dark, he was astonished by what the kits had lead him to. On the cave wall were a mass of red shapes, all outlined in black.

"By all that tugs and tickles the brain!" said Uncle, his jaw dropping open. "Those shapes look remarkably like desert animals! Elephants, look, Radiant – and giraffes!"

"Look at this one!" squealed Little Dream. "It wasn't here before."

"Well I'm bitten!" exclaimed Uncle. The shape he was looking at reminded him of a young Blah-blah male. He was squatting down, pointing with his spear at some tiny pawprints. And behind him, looking at the pawprints too, were… one-two-three-four-five…

"Meerkats!" they all shouted, smiling round at each other. They looked at the picture in silent awe.

"I wonder what's going to happen to them next," whispered Little Dream.

Coming Soon!

Even More Meerkat Madness

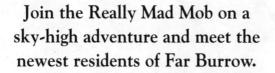

Join the Really Mad Mob on a sky-high adventure and meet the newest residents of Far Burrow.

Have you read?

Meerkat Madness

IAN WHYBROW

It's time to ACT!
We mad little meerkats WILL travel
to see the Blah-Blah mounds and we
SHALL live to tell a tale or two...!

Mimi, Skeema and Little Dream love hearing
tales from their Uncle's glory days – stories
of the Upworld, of befriending blah-blahs and
battling the enemies in the grasses and the skies...
They're just not quite sure they believe him.
But then they find a mysterious object buried
in the sand and it isn't long before they are
caught up in a daring adventure of their own!

Join Uncle and the intrepid pups on their
hilarious journey to Far Burrow.

More animal antics!

FIRST MODERN CLASSICS

Little Wolf's Book of Badness

Ian Whybrow

"A gem of a story."
JEREMY STRONG

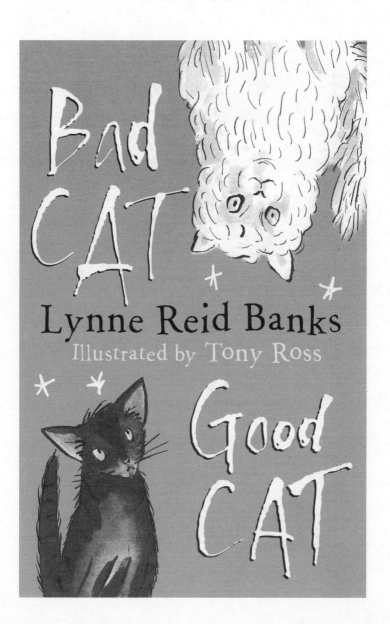

Bad CAT

Lynne Reid Banks

Illustrated by Tony Ross

Good CAT

Coming soon: